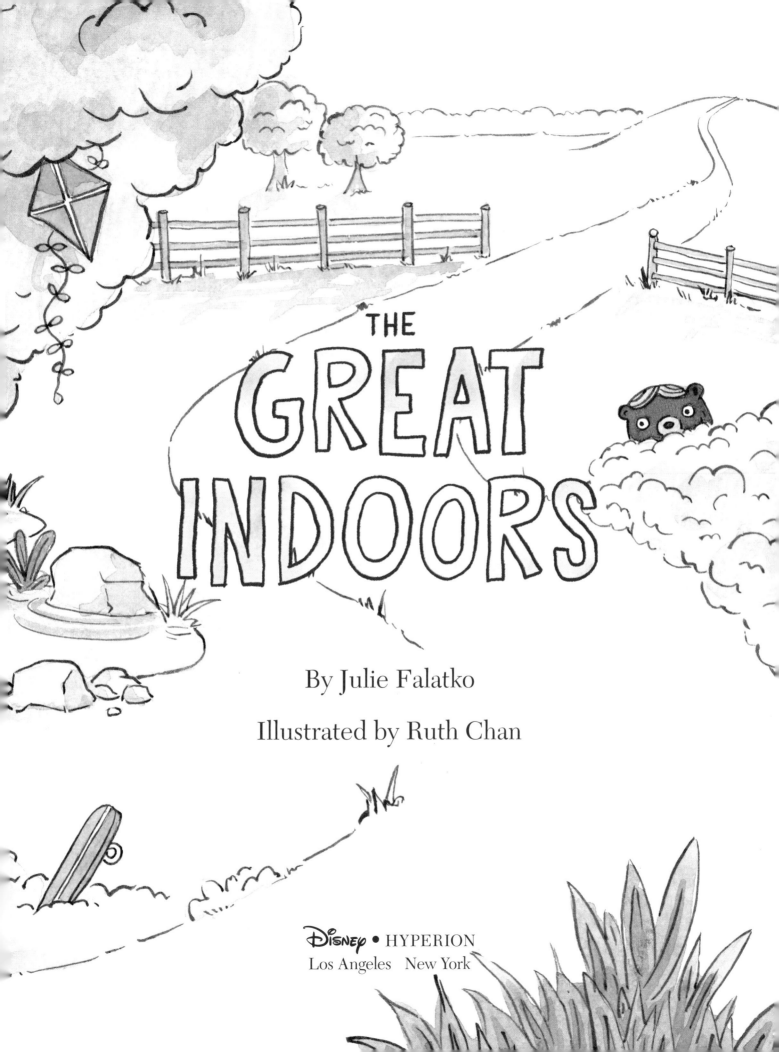

THE GREAT INDOORS

By Julie Falatko

Illustrated by Ruth Chan

DISNEY • HYPERION

Los Angeles   New York

For Dave, who took me camping —J.F.

To my brother, Wes, for exploring the
Great Canadian Outdoors (and Indoors) with me —R.C.

Text copyright © 2019 by Julie Falatko
Illustrations copyright © 2019 by Ruth Chan

First Edition, April 2019
10 9 8 7 6 5 4 3 2 1
FAC-029191-19046

Printed in Malaysia
This book is set in New Caledonia LT Std/Adobe; Chaloops, Garden Gnome/Fontspring.
Designed by Maria Elias and Mary Claire Cruz

Library of Congress Cataloging-in-Publication Data

Names: Falatko, Julie, author. • Chan, Ruth, 1980- illustrator.
Title: The great indoors / by Julie Falatko ; illustrated by Ruth Chan.
Description: First edition. Los Angeles ; New York : Disney-Hyperion, 2019.
Summary: Woodland animals camp in a human house for a weeklong vacation
while the family that lives there is away.
Identifiers: LCCN 2018032599 ISBN 9781368000833 (hardcover)
ISBN 1368000835 (hardcover)
Subjects: CYAC: Vacations—Fiction. Forest animals—Fiction. Humorous stories.
Classification: LCC PZ7.1.F348 Gr 2019 DDC [E]—dc23
LC record available at https://lccn.loc.gov/2018032599

Reinforced binding

Visit www.DisneyBooks.com

The bears always arrived first.

"Ah, the great indoors!"
said the father bear.

"The most relaxing week of the year,"
said the mother bear.

"I call the bathroom!" said the teenage bear,
running in with her blow-dryer and curling iron.

The beavers moved in next,
setting up camp in the kitchen.

"I do so love a roof over my head,"
said one. "Everything stays as dry
as the inside of a pinecone!"

"Here's the ice cream!" said another.
"Shove it all in the freezer before it melts."

The deer were next,
with their karaoke machine.

"Good-bye, peace and quiet!"
said a big deer.

"Hello, dance party!"
said a bigger deer.

The skunks flopped onto the couch.

Everyone gathered around the glow of the television
while the beavers whipped up snacks.

"Can I have more ice in my drink?"
asked the mother bear.

"Of course!"
said the beaver.

"Nothing like a frosty cold drink,"
said the bear. "So much better than the
forest-temperature drinks at home."

"Lasagna time!"
said a beaver in a chef's hat.

The great indoors was the perfect vacation spot.

The bears built things with power tools.

The skunks all enjoyed the excellent cell-phone reception.

The deer crooned love songs and hollered rock anthems.

And the beavers were always ready with

casseroles,

milk shakes,

cookies, and toast.

"I can finally let my hair down," said the big deer.

"I'm going to take another shower!" said a skunk.

As the days went by, things got less than perfect.

STILL
OCCUPIED

The teenage bear still wouldn't come out of the bathroom.

Then it got worse.

Everyone was ready
to go home.

"I miss the peace and quiet,"
said a deer.

"The great indoors is too much work," said a beaver.

"I miss peeing behind a tree," said a little skunk.

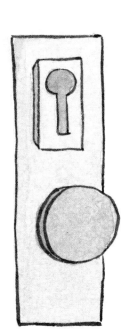